The Bullies and Me

Other Apple Paperbacks you will enjoy:

T.J. and the Pirate Who Wouldn't Go Home
by Carol Gorman

The Cats Nobody Wanted
by Harriet Savitz

Swimmer
by Harriet Savitz

Fast-Talking Dolphin
by Carson Davidson

The Bullies and Me

Harriet Savitz

AN
APPLE
PAPERBACK

SCHOLASTIC INC.
New York Toronto London Auckland Sydney

ISBN 0-590-42975-2

Copyright © 1991 by Harriet May Savitz.
All rights reserved. Published by Scholastic Inc.

APPLE PAPERBACKS is a registered trademark
of Scholastic Inc.

12 11 10 9 8 7 6 5 4 3 2 1   1 2 3 4 5 6/9

Printed in the U.S.A.   40

First Scholastic printing, January 1991

1

I didn't know a thing about ducks until I came to Silver Lake. But lately, I was beginning to care about them a lot, especially the snowbirds. They were the only two white ducks on the lake. Tony told me they had been left on Silver Lake during a snowstorm, and because of that, everybody called them snowbirds. They were smaller than most of the other birds that hung out around the lake. There was something gentle about the way they moved across the water as I watched them.

Tony and Pete didn't seem to care about the ducks at all, except to scare them by making loud noises whenever they were close by. That's why I wasn't anxious to come to Silver Lake with them as much anymore. Even though there were a couple of fish swimming around at the bottom, and even though Pete had a fresh package of marshmallows as bait, I just had one of those feelings that I shouldn't be there, at least not while the lake was crowded with ducks and all the other birds that flew around it, begging for food.

"Hey, look at Big Al and Evelyn." Tony let his fishing pole rest against the railing of the bridge as he pointed toward the street.

The two geese were standing in the middle of the street blocking traffic. We named the male Big Al after a wrestler. He was the darker one. Evelyn was his manager. She kept giving him orders and usually walked behind him, honking as if she were angry at him. The two of them waddled slowly across the street. Even though it took them quite a while to reach the sidewalk on the other side, none of the cars on the street moved.

My grandmom Sarah always worried about Big Al and Evelyn. "Those two are going to get hit by a car if they're not careful," she'd say every time she returned from the lake.

Well, I wasn't as worried about the geese as I was about the different smaller birds that lived on Silver Lake. They usually flew away to visit other places in the summer, but in the fall, like now, they returned to the lake for the long winter. They knew they would be fed by the people in the town. Tony and Pete knew they'd be back, too, and they waited for them. I don't know why but Tony especially liked to bother those ducks.

"Come on," Tony said, losing interest in the fish

that weren't biting at his bait. "Let's clap our hands. Those birds really get scared when you do that."

I would have rather kept fishing. I didn't feel so good inside when the ducks got all excited and flapped their wings. But Tony started hooting and yelling and clapping, and soon the ducks flew away as fast as they could, some swooping over our heads as if they were angry and wanted to get even with us. Others paddled with their webbed feet to the opposite side of the bridge as fast as they could.

Only the geese never got scared, not of Tony or Pete, not of anyone. Evelyn was walking beside Big Al now, coming toward us on the bridge that separated Ocean View from the town of Sea Bright. She was honking real loud as if she were telling Big Al to hurry up. Big Al didn't say much, but when he got angry, he spread his wings and looked twice as big and twice as mean. That's what Big Al was doing now, fanning his wings and heading toward us.

"We'd better get out of here," Pete said, grabbing his fishing rod. Tony didn't like to admit he was afraid of anything. But he didn't like Evelyn or Big Al. And the goose and the gander sure didn't like him. They really didn't like anything but the wooden bridge over the lake where they hung out. If they were in a mean mood, the way they looked today, they'd stand in front of the bridge and not let anyone cross it.

For once I agreed with Tony. I gave my fishing line one more tug, just to make sure there wasn't a fish on the other end. Then I followed Tony off the bridge.

"Those dumb geese can't tell me what to do," Tony grumbled as we walked across the street. "I'm going home," he said. Pete ran behind him. Pete always followed Tony.

I took the shortcut across the park but I still could hear the geese honking. I looked back. Big Al had taken his place at the entrance of the bridge as if he were a tollkeeper waiting for someone to pay him so they could cross over the bridge. I could hear Evelyn and Al honking all the way home.

I didn't understand why everyone in the town put up with Big Al and Evelyn blocking the bridge whenever they felt like it. But then there were a lot of things I didn't understand about this shore town.

We had moved here three months ago, just before I started sixth grade. For me it was a big move because I had never lived anywhere else but on Sandy Hill Road in Mapletown. My dad is a pharmacist. He works for a big chain of stores and they transferred him to Ocean View. The good part for him was that he got a promotion and was made manager. The good part for me was I could run up to the boardwalk and down to the beach to play on the sand anytime I felt like it.

The bad part was that I had to leave all my friends behind; Jimmy and Kevin, but especially David, who had lived across the street from me since I was born. David was one week younger than I was, but we always celebrated our birthdays together.

Today I had an ache in my stomach. The ache came from missing David and all my other friends on Sandy Hill Road. It must have shown on my face.

"What's wrong, Allan? Don't you feel well?" my grandmom asked, feeling my forehead as soon as I had reached home and sat down on the chair next to her on the front porch. "You look just like your mother used to look when she was coming down with a stomach virus."

"I'm okay," I answered.

Grandmom's fingers smelled of garlic and made me wonder what she was making for dinner. I knew Grandmom wasn't having an easy time of it either. Grandpop Harry had died just before we moved. Grandmom Sarah said he fell asleep with a smile on his face and never woke up. So Grandmom came to live with us.

She left behind her friends, too, but she brought

with her everything she and Grandpop owned. All her things, her "treasures," she called them, were packed away in the attic in big brown boxes. No one was allowed to go near them.

"They belong to Harry and me," Grandmom would remind me every time she saw me looking at them. I went up to the attic a lot. I liked being able to look down on the street from so high up.

Grandmom sat next to me on the white rocking chair that was her favorite because it came from the front porch of her own house. She was holding a picture of Grandpop Harry, the one we kept on the living room table. He was sitting on their front porch, wearing his favorite blue jacket. Even in the picture, you could see his thick white hair and clear blue eyes. Grandmom had the same kind of eyes but her hair was thinner.

I missed Grandpop, too. He always played checkers with me when they came to visit. He kept very careful score of how many games each of us won. We'd go for weeks and weeks before he'd add up all the games. Then the loser would buy the winner an ice-cream cone. Whenever Grandpop lost, he'd always buy me a banana split. Nobody played checkers with me anymore.

"Your Grandpop Harry would have loved this place," she said, blowing her nose and wiping her eyes. She always cried when she talked

6

about Grandpop. "It's no fun without him."

I guess Grandmom and I were in the same boat. She wasn't having any fun without Grandpop and I wasn't having any fun without David. Grandmom leaned over and zipped up my jacket. "It's going to be winter soon, Allan. You don't want to catch a chill."

She stood up and I noticed she had her brown bag with her, the one she carried the corn seed in to feed the ducks. "I'm going over to the lake," she said. "Want to come with me?"

I usually took leftover bread even though the pet store owner said corn seed was better for them. I noticed Al and Evelyn always ran for the bread. I guess they were sort of like people, always eating what wasn't good for them.

"I just came from there," I said. The last place I wanted to go today was Silver Lake. Instead I went inside, took a cookie on my way down to the basement, and spent the afternoon putting together another model car for my collection. I had made six cars already, but there was no one around to race them with.

I spent the rest of the week not doing much in school or after it. "I know it's hard making new friends in school," my mother said at breakfast one morning, "but you'll see. One day you'll have a whole new group of friends."

I'm glad *she* believed it. The only thing happening was that when I walked down the hall at Johnson Grammar School, no one even bumped into me. They made big spaces around me. I couldn't tell my mother that.

I spent plenty of time in my room all week. I did sit-ups and push-ups and pull-ups on the rail over my bedroom door. Then each day, I measured myself against the crayoned mark on the wall. My dad was tall. I had his green eyes and red hair. I even had his freckles. My mom was short. I was hoping I would take after my dad's tall side of the family, but it didn't look like that was going to happen.

I kept telling myself all week that it didn't matter if I had no one to play with, or that there was no one in my whole sixth-grade class who understood how great it was to live in Mapletown. Everyone who lived down the shore thought that was the only place to be.

"There's no place better than living near the ocean," Tony once said to me. I didn't think Mapletown was a bad place to live even if it didn't have any water nearby. It had great parks that were miles and miles long and brooks and creeks that ran through them. And Mapletown had a lot of trees. There weren't many trees down the shore.

I didn't really like Pete and Tony, not the way I liked David. I told myself on the way to school that I didn't mind walking alone, and after school, when I was tempted to pick up the telephone to call Tony, I'd remember the ducks and the way Tony teased them. Even from my house, I could hear them quacking on Silver Lake.

I lasted one week, but when Tony finally called and asked me if I wanted to play baseball in the park across from the lake with some of his other friends, I was so lonely I jumped at the chance. "You bet," I said, grabbing my mitt from the bedroom closet. I decided no one was perfect, and Tony and Pete were better than having nobody.

I played first base on Tony's team and hit two home runs. After the game, everybody from both teams ran down to the beach. The tourists had left and we had it all to ourselves. I had come to Ocean View at the end of the summer. The beaches were still crowded and the weather was warm. I had never been to the beach when it got cold and was empty. It was like having a big playground all to ourselves.

"Come on, Allan." One of the boys from the other team called me over as if he and I were old friends. "Let's make a sand castle."

We began digging up wet sand near the water, piling it in clumps over the castle, which was getting higher. I felt good being part of the group, even though they were all Tony's friends, kids he had grown up with. Most of them were twelve, a year older than I was.

It was one of those afternoons I wished would last forever. The sky was blue with puffy clouds standing still overhead. The ocean was clear. I could see right through the waves when they rolled over. Sometimes the ocean was dirty with garbage, and a few times this summer the beaches had been closed and we couldn't swim; but today it looked sparkling clean. Some of the sea gulls, and there must have been about twenty of them, were standing on one leg, watching us build our castle. Once in a while, one of them would fly out over the ocean, swoop down into one of the waves, and get some dinner. Then the air would fill with the sound of their screams, as if they were laughing out loud.

When it was time to go home, Tony, Pete, and I walked back together. We took the shortcut down past the lake. I didn't even mind that today. Everything was so still and peaceful. The green-necked mallards were quiet, too, just gliding slowly by the bridge. Even Evelyn and Big Al were in a good mood. They didn't even honk as they stood on the grass watching us go by. The two snowbirds were resting under the willow tree where they usually hung out.

Tony had left the grass on the side of the lake and was making his way over the large rocks near the water.

"Come on," he waved to us.

Pete and I ran down to the edge of the water. It was fun trying to keep our balance over the wet rocks. Tony bent down and picked up some stones. He threw one into the lake and one of the white ducks fluttered her wings.

"I bet you can't hit one of those ducks," Tony said, handing me a stone.

Well the last thing I wanted to do was try.

"What do you want to hit one of the ducks for?" I asked Tony.

He looked at me as if I had said something stupid. "What, are you *afraid*, Allan? You afraid of the ducks?"

Pete already had a handful of stones. He was tossing them, one after the other, high into the air. Each one would make a plunking sound as it hit the water. If there was a duck nearby, it would fly away. Ducks were smart that way.

"Maybe we just won't call you anymore when we go to the beach," Tony said, his dark eyes challenging me. "You're scared to do anything."

This afternoon at the beach, for the first time, I had the feeling that I wasn't the new kid in town. That's the way I was always introduced. But today I felt as if I belonged, just the way I did back

11

on Sandy Hill Road in Mapletown. I didn't want to lose that feeling over a couple of ducks. I took a stone and, aiming carefully so I wouldn't hit anything, I tossed it into the water. Pete threw a few more and so did Tony. Before I knew it, we were all throwing stones faster and faster as we ran alongside the lake.

The faster the stones hit the water, the quicker the lake cleared of birds. All except the two snowbirds. They slowly made their way around the rocks near the side of the hill. The stones were plopping close by their white feathers.

I stopped throwing when I saw that the larger duck looked like he was in trouble. He wasn't moving as fast as the other white duck. Now and then the smaller bird would slow down as if it were waiting for the slower one, who was barely moving forward.

"Do you think he got hurt by one of the stones?" I asked. My voice sounded scared, the way it did sometimes when I had a bad dream and woke up in the middle of the night. I was glad Tony and Pete weren't even paying any attention to me. They were running as fast as they could, trying to beat each other up the block.

I just stood there for a long time by the side of the lake watching the larger snowbird slowly make his way toward the bridge. I could tell it was hurting. There was something about the way it fluttered its wings now and then, as if it was having trouble balancing itself.

I didn't want it to be true, but I knew in my heart, the larger snowbird had been hit by one of the stones. All the way home I wondered which stone, and was I the one who threw it.

2

Grandmom Sarah told me a few days later what I already knew.

"People can be so cruel sometimes," she said. She was sitting on the couch in front of the television set, her knitting needles clicking back and forth. I never knew how she could work on the sweater she was making me and watch television and talk at the same time.

"I just don't understand," she said, shaking her head as she bent down and dug into her knitting bag. She handed me a twisted pile of wool. "Here," she said. "Keep yourself busy and get the knots out."

Grandmom had a habit of waiting when she had something important to say, until I'd almost bust from wanting to know the story. I knew what she was waiting for. She wanted me to ask, "What do you mean?" I liked the way Grandmom told a story. She usually took more time than my mom and dad, who were always busy doing something in the house.

14

"What do you mean?" I asked. I sat on the floor trying to untwist the blue wool.

"One of the snowbirds on Silver Lake died. Its wing was broken and it just suffered away."

I could have done without *this* story. In fact, I was sort of hoping she was finished telling it and had nothing more to say about the snowbird.

"Someone said they saw a bunch of kids throwing rocks the day before it died. Guess the male snowbird was hit. He was the bigger one. Such a shame. He was such a pretty bird. Now the female is all alone."

"You don't know it was hit by some rocks!" I surprised myself by yelling. "It could have gotten sick or something."

Grandmom looked down at me over her eyeglasses. "Getting sick doesn't break your wing. Didn't mean to get you so upset," she said, her blue eyes digging into me.

"I'm not upset," I answered. I dropped the tangled wool back into her knitting bag, then left the living room. I could feel Grandmom's gaze following me all the way up the stairs to my bedroom.

I had the snowbird on my mind all night. I looked out the window and stared toward the direction of the lake. I couldn't see the ducks but I knew they were all puffed up, sleeping, all but one of them. He wasn't there anymore.

The next day when I went to school, I told Tony

15

what my grandmother had said. He didn't seem interested.

"We're going to the video arcade," he told me. "Meet you there."

It made me feel better, thinking about the video arcade. We didn't have anything like the Ocean Arcade in Mapletown. This arcade was right on the boardwalk facing the ocean, and it was open all year around. I decided Tony wasn't so bad after all, asking me to go.

Tony was at the video games when I got there, since I had to stay after school to make up a test. I went right to the bowling. It wasn't like regular bowling with big black balls. David and I used to bowl a lot on Saturdays. These were little wooden balls, and I had won plenty of coupons by getting the balls into the circles marked 25, 50, 150, and 200. Each circle got smaller and smaller as the points got higher. But today, as I stood there, I just didn't feel like putting my money into the slot to begin the game. I looked down at the change in my hand I had left over from my allowance and decided I had something more important to do with it.

There was a telephone booth right outside the arcade. I dropped the coins inside the machine and dialed David, long distance.

"Hello, David," I said as soon as he answered. "It's me."

"Hey Allan! You calling me all the way from Ocean View?"

"Yeah," I answered. "You hear the ocean?" I put the telephone out toward the beach for a few seconds.

"I hear it!" David said, his voice all excited. "I wanted to call you last week a couple of times, but my mom said it was long distance and would cost a lot of money. She told me to write you a letter."

"I'm using my allowance money," I told David. "I'm standing on the boardwalk, right next to the arcade."

"Boy, you're lucky, Allan. You have that all year 'round."

"Yeah, I guess I am," I answered. I didn't say anything about Tony or the ducks. I knew David wouldn't approve.

"You should be glad you're not here," David said. "I got old lady Block for English. Every night she gives a load of homework. And she makes you write these long compositions."

I didn't want to talk about old lady Block or school. "You want to come down here some time?" I asked David. "Maybe for a weekend?"

I wanted to ask David about the maple tree in my backyard on Sandy Hill Road. It would always be my maple tree, no matter who lived in that house. I bet the leaves were all over the backyard

17

like an orange and yellow blanket. I thought I wouldn't even mind raking them up like I used to do every year about this time.

"Did the leaves fall from the maple tree yet?" I asked.

"Your three minutes are up," the operator told me. "Please deposit forty-five cents if you wish to talk longer."

"I don't have forty-five cents," I told David quickly.

"I'll ask my mom about coming down," David answered before I hung up.

The phone call had cost me one dollar. I decided to put that money away each week from my allowance, even if it meant less visits to the arcade, just so I could talk to one of my friends from Mapletown. I felt so much better now after hearing David's voice.

But my good mood didn't last long. No one else felt good at my house that night. There was a lot of grumbling going on at the kitchen table and soon David seemed very far away.

"Where's your mother?" my dad asked Mom. He looked tired. He had dark circles around his eyes and he was yawning a lot.

"She's in the attic," Mom answered. "You look exhausted, George. I don't know why you have to work so much overtime."

My dad just grumbled. "A lot of people have the flu."

After dinner Mom made our lunch sandwiches and put them in the refrigerator. She worked as a secretary in a real estate office on Main Street, so she always made our lunches the night before. Dad washed the dishes. I dried.

"Why does Grandmom spend so much time in that attic?" Dad asked as he stacked the dishes in the drainer. "She was up there yesterday, too, when I came home from work."

"That's where all her things are," my mother answered. "She misses my dad. I guess she just feels closer to him when she goes through the things in those boxes." My mom's face got sad. She fingered the gold necklace Gramps had given her right before he died. "He would have loved to live near the ocean," she said so quietly I don't think my dad even heard her.

"She should just get rid of that stuff," my dad muttered, handing me a glass with soap bubbles sliding down the outside. We didn't have a built-in dishwasher in this house yet, and Dad never rinsed the dishes enough. I handed him back the glass. "Most of that junk she'll never use anyway. Maybe we'll have a big garage sale in the spring," he said.

"Mom would never get rid of her books," my

mother said. "What would an ex-librarian be without them?" Then she went over to my dad and put her arm around his shoulder. "My, you are in a bad mood tonight," she said. "Can I help?"

"I'm sorry," my dad answered, handing me another glass. "It's the job. Everyone is used to the old boss, Bob, and *his* ways. That's all I hear all day: 'Bob never did it that way.' "

"They'll forget him," my mom said. "Give it a little time. Gradually he'll just fade away."

That idea didn't make me feel so good. I wondered if David and all my friends back in Mapletown would do the same, if they would forget what I looked like. I wanted to bring up the sleepover that I had been talking to David about, but it didn't seem to be the right time.

Mom opened the freezer and stood there for a while. "Anybody have ideas on what they'd like for dinner tomorrow night?"

I knew she always had to be a day ahead to defrost whatever she needed for dinner so that it was ready when she got home from work. She usually got home before Dad.

Nobody answered. It was tough thinking about tomorrow's dinner when we'd just finished dinner tonight.

After the kitchen was cleaned, Dad and I carried the newspapers down into the basement. This town had a recycling plant, so we had to separate the garbage. The newspapers were picked up twice a month.

On the way up the stairs, Dad knocked his head against the ledge that hung over the steps. Dad was so tall he had to bend in order to miss it, and he always forgot.

"Darn this place," he said, rubbing his forehead.

I looked up at the ledge and hoped some day I'd grow tall enough to knock my head, too.

I spent a lot of time that week after school riding my bicycle on the boardwalk. Even though it was empty, and the tourists had all left, there were a lot of sea gulls on the beach to keep me company. They were sitting on the boardwalk railings, too. I was used to seeing them everywhere, on telephone poles near the boardwalk, and at the bay, sitting on the pier waiting for the fishermen to throw them some leftover bait. Grandmom said they were the scavengers of the sea and that they kept it clean. They could follow a ship for hundreds of miles, eating up everything that was thrown out from the kitchen. At least that's what Grandmom said.

That day when I got home, the Welcome Wagon station wagon was in front of our house. Inside, there was a lady talking with my mother in the kitchen. Sitting on one of the chairs was Flute. I recognized him right away. That wasn't his real name. His real name was Alexander, but everyone in the school called him "Flute" because he was a flutist in the school band.

"Do you know Alexander Greenwood?" my mother asked, introducing us. "This is my son, Allan."

"Hi, Allan," Flute said.

"Hi," I answered. I didn't think his mother would appreciate it if I called him Flute, so I didn't call him anything.

Flute's mother and my mother seemed to be having a good time, drinking tea and talking in the kitchen. Flute didn't have anything to say to me, and I didn't have anything to say to him, so we just sat there, drinking milk and eating up the cookies on the plate in front of us as fast as we could.

"He seems like such a nice boy," my mom said when they left. "Now there's somebody who would make a nice friend. Jeanie, his mother, will be coming over again. What a nice woman. She brought me little gifts from the Welcome Wagon, to welcome me into the community. What a nice lady," my mother said again.

I was glad my mother had found someone she liked, but I really wasn't anxious to be Flute's friend. He hung out with the kids in the band. Everyone else always made fun of the "bandies." Sometimes when Flute would walk by I'd see one of the kids move their fingers as if they were playing an imaginary flute. Flute did a lot of things that were different from everyone else. He always wore shirts and bow ties, and he was always carrying his flute around in a black case.

I didn't go to Silver Lake all week and was just beginning to forget about the snowbird when Grandmom brought it up again. It was getting cold out. There was a frost in the morning and the clouds looked like dark mountains hanging over the ocean. The ocean had turned gray and it got dark before five o'clock, so we had to be off the boardwalk before then.

I was walking with Grandmom one day to Virgil's grocery store to pick up a loaf of bread and some popcorn — Grandmom loved her popcorn when she watched television at night — when she suddenly headed toward the lake.

I tried to steer her in the opposite direction. "Why do we have to walk by the lake?" I asked. "Let's take the shortcut home across the park."

"I want to check on Snowbird," she said. "Do you know she hasn't left the area since her mate died? Poor thing. Those little white ducks were probably dropped off by someone who had them as pets."

"Why doesn't she just go live somewhere else?"

I asked. "Maybe she'd be happier living at another lake." I knew I would be happier if she found another home.

"Most of the ducks on this lake won't fly far," Grandmom answered. "They are domesticated and have lost the instinct to migrate. They're not such strong flyers because they've been doing so much sitting around. If no one feeds Snowbird, she'll starve. She considers this place home. She's really stranded on Silver Lake."

I couldn't stand the thought of it. That meant I never again would be able to go to the lake without wondering if it was one of my stones that hit her mate, and I would always have to be looking at Snowbird, thinking how lonely she must be. I wished she could just pick up and relocate the way we did when we came to the shore.

When we got to the lake all the ducks were gone, except Snowbird, who was cleaning herself under the willow tree. As soon as she saw Grandmom and me, she jumped into the lake. Grandmom reached into her pocket and scattered some corn seed into the water.

"I always carry some with me," she explained, taking more from her coat pocket.

"The others must have flown off to visit for the day," Grandmom said. "Sometimes they fly to a nearby lake if there isn't enough food around." She peeked in the green house that was at the top of the ramp that went from the lake to the hill. Sometimes the ducks would gather around it and even go inside when the weather was bad. "Nope. No one in there, either," she said. Then she looked down at the ground and frowned.

"Look at this place, will you? No wonder they left. This lake area is a mess."

There were boxes of garbage floating around the sides of the lake. It looked dirty on top, sort of yellowish instead of clear blue. When you looked down into it, the water wasn't clear. Instead of looking down at the dirty water, it was more fun to look at the houses in Sea Bright, on the other side of the bridge. They were like tall castles with lots of windows, and there was a whole row of them facing Ocean View. Every house was a different color and they stood on the other side of the lake as if they were watching us.

Grandmom scattered some more seeds on the ground around the green shed. "There aren't the tourists in the winter to feed the ducks," she told me. Then she looked up at the sky. "The winter is in the clouds already," she said.

Grandmom was right about that. The winter came down on Ocean View in one big, cold blast of wind that was so strong it sent the signs on the boardwalk banging in the wind, and the sand blew all over the sidewalk, even two and three blocks inland. I couldn't even walk up to the boardwalk for two weeks. The winds were so strong they took my breath away and blew stinging sand into my eyes.

I kept myself busy inside the house doing push-ups. I pulled myself up on the thick rope that was tied to my bedroom doorknob thirty-five times in one workout. When I looked in the mirror to measure myself, I didn't notice a change, except that I seemed to have more freckles on my face.

Even though the salt air always made me hungry and my appetite seemed to be increasing, Grandmom's news bulletins took my appetite away.

"Snowbird is having a tough time," she said yesterday. "It's so cold out and none of the other ducks are going near her. It's a shame. She just glides about in her own space and you can tell she misses her mate. She's so lonely."

The news bulletins came at least once a day. I wanted to tell Grandmom I wasn't interested in her snowbird stories, but I couldn't say anything like that to Grandmom Sarah. She cried real easy and the only time she seemed happy was when she was telling me stories. So I just let her talk and I tried to think of other things, like how I'd wake up one morning and find myself back on Sandy Hill Road in Mapletown, living next door to David again.

3

"We're just going to have a wonderful time today," my mother said as we waited on the porch for Jeanie Greenwood and her son, Flute. They were going to pick us up and take us to the mall. Our mothers were going to go shopping for sheets and towels at a big white sale at Brenner's department store.

I wasn't too anxious to spend a day with Flute, especially a Saturday when Tony and Pete usually had something planned, but my mom had made up her mind that Flute would be a good friend for me and I wasn't about to tell her that I didn't think I had anything in common with a flute player. When Mom made up her mind to do something, she wouldn't change it until she was ready.

We were both pretty quiet during the ride, but once Flute and I got to the mall and were on our own, we found a lot of things to do. Some of them I had never done before.

"I have to pick up some flute music," Flute said.

I had never been to a music store before. There was piano music and guitar music, sheets and sheets of it.

"I'll just be a couple of minutes," Flute said. "I know what I want."

I went up and down the aisles, looking at the music of the songs I knew. I couldn't imagine anyone playing those notes on a flute. When Flute was finished, we went to the hobby shop. I wanted to get another model car to put together. Flute was real interested as we sorted through the boxes.

"I never worked on one of these," he said.

I couldn't imagine someone who had never put together a model car. "My dad and I do them all the time. We usually keep our models on a shelf in the basement. Sometimes we race them together." Lately my dad didn't have much time for racing, but I didn't tell Flute that.

I finally picked out a Porsche with four fancy tires, white top, and black windows. It had batteries and a special engine, four-wheel drive and was great for racing.

"How do you put it together?" Flute asked.

"It depends," I told him. "Sometimes we get a tube of grease and you slide the parts into place. Sometimes they just snap into place. But there're lots of parts and you have to know what you're doing."

Flute stood there staring at the boxes of model cars on the shelf. He looked like I looked sometimes when I was in Virgil's grocery store, staring at the candy bars that I wanted to eat.

"You want to make one of the cars?" I asked.

Flute's face just about lit up. His dark eyes got wider. "Boy, that would be neat," he said. Then he shook his head. "I don't know if I could do it alone."

"Couldn't your dad help you?" I asked.

"My dad travels a lot," Flute answered. But he said it as if he didn't mind that at all. "And besides, I never saw him do anything like this. He's a musician. He plays the piano in a band."

Well, I did the only polite thing I could do. "I guess I could help you do your first one," I answered.

That's all Flute needed to hear. He picked out a Porsche. His had a red top with white windows.

We decided that since he would be working on his first model car with me, we would keep it downstairs in my cellar and work on it there. We spent the whole day in our basement and I had to admit it was more fun putting the cars together while talking to someone else. It made the time go faster.

I guess Flute thought that because we were working on the cars together, we were friends. When I was eating lunch at school, he'd come over with his lunch. Or when I was walking to my locker, he would catch up with me. "Allan, can we work after school on the cars?" he'd ask. One day he even said, "I told my dad about it and he said if I learn how to put them together, he might try one with me someday."

Well, that was pretty good news to me. I didn't want to be stuck putting model cars together with Flute for the rest of my life, even though it probably would have made my mother very happy.

At the end of the week, there was a special assembly in school. The school band played all the new songs they had learned and Flute did a solo on his flute. He sounded pretty good up there on the stage of the auditorium, and he didn't seem afraid to be playing in front of so many people.

"Hey, are you Flute's friend?" Tony asked when we walked out of the assembly. Tony laughed as he pretended he was playing the flute.

I didn't think it would do me any good to answer yes. "Are you kidding?" I said. "His mother is on the Welcome Wagon. She's friendly with my mom. She just keeps bringing him over to the house with her."

"You poor kid," Tony said. "What a creep to have to spend time with."

Actually, though I didn't tell Tony, Flute wasn't such a creep. In fact, he learned quickly how to put the model car together. For some reason, I didn't feel so good about myself after I said that to Tony.

One evening I brought my car upstairs to show my dad. He was sort of snoozing in the big soft-back chair in the living room.

"That looks great, Allan," he said, holding it up to the light. "I really miss doing that with you. I just wish I had the time."

Dad and I used to do a lot of things together back in Mapletown. We played basketball just about every evening. We had a net in the drive-way and there was a big light on the side so we could go out there even when it was dark. Here we didn't have anything in the driveway but two parked cars. Dad was always promising to put up a net. I wanted to ask him about it now, but I didn't think it was the right time.

"I'm having problems at work," he said while he examined the car. "It just takes getting used to the people I'm working with." He sounded as if he were waiting for me to say something to make him feel better.

I didn't know what to say since I was having the same kind of problems at school. I guess I couldn't help my dad with his problems and he couldn't help me with mine. Flute had become one of my problems.

I didn't mind being with Flute now and then on

Saturdays, when I had nothing else to do, because our model car collection was building up and we even managed to race them one day in the driveway, but he was beginning to hang around me at school, as if he expected to go with me when I was with Pete and Tony. In fact, everyone was beginning to think of me as Flute's friend.

"Where's Flute today?" someone would ask me when Flute was out sick. One day the music teacher even asked, "Allan, when you see Flute will you tell him I want to see him."

But on the day of the big snowstorm, nothing seemed important except getting to the beach with everyone else on the block. The sand was covered with ice. We even had the day off from school. There were over six inches of snow covering the sidewalk.

I went up to the attic to get out my sled. I had to walk up two long flights to get there. It was a walk-in attic, much bigger than the one we had in Mapletown. When we moved here, Dad said someday we could make it into a guest room, it was that big.

It was cold in the attic, much colder than the rest of the house. I guessed it was because of the strong winds that were blowing the snow from one side of the street to the other. Just as I found my sled toward the back of the attic, I noticed that there was a window open a few inches and bits of snow were flying into the attic. I pushed some boxes away until I reached it. It was one of those old windows that you have to push down real hard on, but I finally got it closed.

"Hi, Allan. What are you doing up here?"

I tell you, I was so surprised, I nearly dropped the sled on my foot. Grandmom was sitting there on the floor, wrapped up in her heavy winter coat, stacking books on the floor.

"I came to get my sled," I told her, staring down at the boxes that were opened. They all had books inside.

"From my library days," Grandmom explained, noticing what I was looking at. "I collected hundreds of them when I was a librarian. No room here to put them anywhere and I just can't part with them. So I come upstairs now and then to visit them."

I knew a lot of things I'd save when I got older. My model cars, for one. And probably all my games, especially the Monopoly set. But I didn't think I'd save my books, at least not that many, and by the stacks of boxes there looked to be over a hundred.

"These are Grandpop's things." Grandmom pulled over a long box to her feet. She sniffed a few times and blew her nose into a handkerchief. Instead of closing the box the way she usually did when I was around, she kept it open. "I miss him so," she said, picking up a woolen scarf and smoothing the wrinkles from it. "You know, no one tells you how to get over missing someone. Not that I'd want to." She picked up a small stuffed bear from the box. It was gray with black beaded eyes. "This was Grandpop's," she said. "He bought it for your mother when she was born. Then, when she was finished playing with it, he decided to keep it himself. Imagine that. He was such a gentle man." She looked at me. "I think he'd want you to have it."

I didn't want to tell Grandmom I was too old for bears. Instead, I took it. It felt as if it belonged in my arms as I held it.

"Aren't you cold?" I asked Grandmom.

"My memories keep me warm," she answered.

I stood there for a few minutes, not knowing what to say, not wanting to be rude, while Grandmom looked over old photographs and Grandpop's winter hats and gloves. She had even packed away his eyeglasses and his pipe. Finally I said, "I've got to get going, Grandmom. Tony and Pete are waiting for me."

"Make sure you dress warm," Grandmom called after me.

I met Tony and Pete near the boardwalk. I had never gone sledding on a beach before.

"The snow always melts real fast down here," Tony said, his dark eyes all excited. "The ocean keeps the air warmer. But today, it's great. It's freezing all over."

It wasn't easy getting down to the beach with all the snow on the boardwalk. No one had shoveled or cleared a pathway, so we had to push our boots through it, making our own trail.

Pete was already on the beach. I watched him with his blue snow cap run a few feet, then flop on the sled down the slope toward the ocean. I had to admit I had never been able to do anything like this in Mapletown. The waves were beating against the jetties and the sun was warm, almost like it gets in the spring, even though the air was so cold my breath made smoke rings. It was the greatest feeling gliding down the beach toward the water, seeing the waves tumbling around in front of me, then stopping a few feet from where they broke.

"There's your friend, Flute," Tony said, with a smirk on his face. "He's with the bandies."

That's what they called the guys who played in the band. They looked as if they were having a good time, too.

Then, I don't know how it happened, but they were sledding closer to us and we to them and before I knew it, Tony and Pete and a few from our group were throwing snowballs in Flute's direction. Flute and his friends started throwing them back.

35

The snowballs got bigger and harder and the throwing faster. I didn't feel right about being on the opposite side to Flute, or watching him get hit with one snowball after another as Tony aimed right at him. As I stood there, I remembered the snowbird and the stones I had thrown. Suddenly, I didn't want to throw snowballs anymore.

"I've got to get home," I told Tony. "My mom wants me to shovel the sidewalk." That part was true. I didn't tell Tony I could have done it later. I took my sled and went home.

That night, when I went into my bedroom, I was thinking about all the things I didn't like about this house. It had smaller rooms than our old house. My mother didn't like that either. She told my father last night there was no space for walking in the house. My dad said it was the best we could afford. And it had radiators instead of vents. Whenever the heat was on, the radiators made noise, a hissing sound that woke me up through the night. And sometimes if we didn't empty the heater downstairs, the water would shoot out of the radiators and spill onto the floor. My mother had a little glass dish underneath each radiator just in case it leaked.

There was another thing wrong with the house. It wasn't straight. If you spilled anything on the floor, it rolled from one side of the room to the other as if we were standing on a hill. Even the windows were crooked.

I took the bear that Grandmom had given me from the bed and plunked it on top of my desk. He looked straight at me as if he knew what I was thinking.

I was thinking, Why couldn't things stay the way they were last year? I guess the lonely snowbird was thinking the same thing.

4

David was coming today to Ocean View, during our Christmas vacation. His parents were driving him down and they would visit with my parents. My parents would drive him home the next day.

All morning I made plans for the visit. David and I would spend the afternoon at the arcade, and after dinner — which would be our favorite, pizza and French fries — we'd get into a game of Monopoly. And then we'd talk all night. I didn't intend to sleep one minute. Tony and Pete didn't do much talking, but David liked to talk about everything. We'd talk about if there was life anywhere on other planets, and we'd talk about being astronauts, and we'd even talk about girls. Not much, but sometimes.

My dad peeked his head in through the doorway. He had a big smile on his face. "Today's the big day," he said. "You'd better clean up this mess, Allan. David won't have a place to sleep."

He was right. My dad and I had brought a cot down from the attic. But it was still folded in the corner because my clothes were all over the floor. I spent a good hour in my room cleaning up. I even found some single socks under the bed. I knew my mom would be glad about that since she was always looking for the other sock to a pair.

"What do you do Allan, eat them?" she'd ask.

If you asked me, I'd say the washing machine ate them. That's where they all seemed to get lost.

When I finally came downstairs, I walked right into a battle between Mom and Grandmom Sarah.

"I don't believe you did it," my grandmom said. She was sitting in the chair near the front door. She had on her blue hat, the special one she wore when she went out to visit. But she wasn't wearing her visiting face. Instead she looked angry. "Why would you do such a thing?"

My mom had an answer for her. "Well, I told the lady at the library about all your library experience and she was really impressed. She said they always need volunteers to do cataloging of new books and they would so appreciate your coming in to talk to them about it. It just seemed the natural thing to do, to make the appointment for you while I was there." Mom glanced at the clock. "You should really get going."

Grandmom just glared back at Mom. She had

her arms folded in front of her and, I noticed, she didn't have her knitting bag in her lap.

. My mom didn't give up. "Look, Mother, it's only a few blocks away. You could walk it or use my car if you want to. It's a great-looking library, inside. I know you'd feel comfortable there."

Grandmom didn't look as if she would be comfortable anywhere today. She stood up, then sat down, as if she was going then staying, all at the same time.

My mom's voice got soft, the way it sometimes got when I was hurt, like the time I was riding my bike and fell off it, skinning my knees. She took hold of Grandmom's hands. "You know how much I love you and how it hurts for me to see you up there in the attic all the time. Dad wouldn't want you sitting around like this, not for a minute. You know he wouldn't."

I could tell by Grandmom's face that was definitely the wrong thing for my mom to say. Grandmom took the long hat pin out of her hat and plopped the hat down on the table next to the door. "Young lady, I'm grown up. I don't need anyone planning my day or telling me what to do with it. And certainly no one can tell me what Harry would have wanted because nobody knows Harry better than I do."

She marched over to the telephone and dialed a number. "This is Sarah Jenkins," she said.

"Please tell Mary Koller that I can't come in today. I'll call her again to make another appointment."

Grandmom slammed down the telephone. My mom and I listened to her footsteps going all the way up the stairs to the attic. I didn't expect what happened next. My mom sat down on the living room couch and began to cry.

"Mom?" I asked.

My mom stopped crying, sniffled a few times, then just sat there, looking kind of lonely. "Oh, Allan, things just keep piling up. Dad's job is giving him problems. Grandmom is so unhappy. And I guess I just miss Grandpop," she said. "If he were here, he'd know what to do with Grandmom. He'd know what to do about a lot of things. He was always so good at solving problems, wasn't he?"

I knew he was good at playing checkers. I didn't know what to say to my mom, so I just reached into my pocket and handed her a stick of chewing gum. That seemed to help because she smiled at me as she unwrapped it.

When the phone rang, I thought maybe it was the lady from the library calling back. I wasn't expecting the voice I heard.

"Hello, Allan. This is David."

David sounded as if he were talking from a basement. "How come you're not on your way?" I asked.

David sneezed for an answer. I heard him blow his nose at the other end of the telephone.

"I'm sick," he said.

"You can't be sick," I told him. "It's our Christmas vacation!"

"I'm not too happy about it either," he said, sneezing again. "You think I like laying in bed here, with my mom giving me that terrible stuff she thinks helps all colds . . . honey and tea? I'm sorry, Allan."

Why did he have to be sick today? I thought. But I knew it wasn't really his fault. "I guess you couldn't help it," I said. "Maybe you'll feel better tomorrow. Maybe you could come out then."

I waited a minute or two while David coughed. "I don't think so," he said. "My stomach doesn't feel too good either."

"Oh," I answered. By then, I wasn't feeling too good myself. "Well, look, David," I said. "We'll do it another time." I tried not to let my disappointment show. "At least we know our parents will drive us back and forth."

David sneezed again and, in between coughs, said good-bye.

"Who was that?" my mom asked when I came back into the living room.

"David's not coming," I answered. "He has a cold."

"Oh, what a shame," my mom said. She put her

arm around me. "But I'll tell you the truth, Allan, it just might be for the best. We have so much to do around the house during this vacation, to catch up."

Mom wasn't kidding about that either. That night she told Dad and me everything that was wrong with the house. "The floor creaks. There's a leak in the pipe downstairs. All of the plumbing is going to have to be changed. And the roof leaks. It's just old . . . old . . . old," she said, and I thought she was going to cry again. Back in Mapletown we never talked about the house. It never caused us any trouble. This place never stopped groaning and making noises.

Later, Dad and I went down to the basement to finish painting it so the rainwater wouldn't come through the cellar walls. Dad didn't look any happier about doing it than I did.

"Are you sorry we moved here?" my dad asked. The question sort of surprised me. He looked so sad, I didn't have the heart to tell him the truth.

"It's great being near the ocean," I said. That much wasn't a lie.

"I think your mom is sorry. And Grandmom sure is. I guess no one is happy with what I've done," Dad said. He was making high white strokes across the part of the wall I couldn't reach. "I thought I was doing the right thing for all of us."

I had a feeling this was a conversation Dad really wanted to have with Mom.

"There's no going back, Allan, not after a decision like this," he went on. "I'm really beginning to like the job. It pays more and there's a good chance for advancement. And this old house," Dad touched the walls with his hands, "I sort of like it. It has personality."

A few minutes later he forgot about the "personality" as he walked up the stairs. "Ouch," he said, knocking his head against the ledge.

I had gone through a lot of winters in Mapletown, but I never went through a January like we had down the shore. When the winds didn't blow me off the boardwalk, the ice made it so slippery I couldn't walk. There was a sleet storm and the temperatures dipped below freezing and the ice stayed and stayed. It just wouldn't melt.

Grandmom was very careful when she walked down the front steps to go for her walk. I helped her whenever I was home. One day when the sun was real bright and most of the ice had left the streets, Grandmom asked me to go with her for a walk on the boardwalk. "I'd still feel better not walking alone today," she said. "There are still bits of ice on the street."

I didn't tell her, but I didn't like to walk alone, either. Most of the time when I was with Tony and Pete and their friends, we were doing something. No one but Grandmom just liked to walk and talk and tell stories.

We walked very slowly down the street, where it was shoveled and clear, up toward the boardwalk. For a while we stood by the railing, staring at the sea gulls squatting on the beach. The ocean's waves looked as if they had been polished with silver. It almost hurt my eyes to look at them. The bright sunlight did that to the ocean.

"Do you know, years ago women trimmed their hats with gull's wings," Grandmom told me. "We lost thousands of these birds because of that. Then the Audubon Society said the massacre must stop, and now we have laws to protect the sea gull. Now there are paid keepers who patrol some of the islands where gulls nest."

We sat down on a bench. The sun was hot. It seemed out of place when everything was so cold around us.

"The gulls are such beautiful scavengers of the sea," Grandmom said. "They clean the ocean for us, do you know that, Allan? Though goodness knows, I'm certain the sea gulls didn't count on it being so polluted. Do you know they've been known to follow an ocean liner across the entire Atlantic Ocean? They use the waves as their bed to refresh themselves at night." I didn't want to tell her she had told me that story before. Grandmom liked to repeat some stories and I didn't mind listening to them over and over again.

I laid my head back on the bench and closed my eyes. The sun felt warm and made me tired. I didn't even notice that Grandmom had left the bench until I heard her call my name. I turned around just in time to see her legs buckle under and her arms go reaching toward the sky. I jumped right off the bench and ran, but by the time I got to Grandmom, she was lying flat on the boardwalk.

"It's okay, Allan. It's okay," she said. "I think I might just have turned my ankle."

Grandmom's face was real pale. "Can you get up?" I asked, starting to wonder how I was going to get her home.

Grandmom leaned on me and hobbled over to the bench. "Why don't you go back and get your mother," she said. "I'll wait right here. I'll be fine."

I didn't want to leave her, but I knew I wasn't doing her any good standing there. I bet I beat Tony's record down that street. Mom drove the car back and between us we managed to get Grandmom into the car.

"I'm driving right to the doctor," my mom said when she dropped me off at the house.

"I don't know what all the fuss is about," Grandmom interrupted, though she looked like she was in pain.

I was worried about Grandmom and, sitting staring at the clock on my bureau wondering what was going on in the doctor's office, wasn't doing me any good. Any company was better than no company. I went to the telephone and called Tony. "What are you doing?" I asked.

"Watching television," he answered.

"Want to come over?" I said.

"Sure," he answered.

We decided to throw darts. The dart set was on the back of my bedroom door. I had forgotten about the bear Grandmom had given me. It was lying on top of the bureau and Tony noticed it right away.

"You got to be kidding," he said. "You still have that baby stuff?" He picked it up and wagged it back and forth. The bear's head plopped around. Its neck didn't look too strong but I guessed it had been played with a lot over all the years.

"It's just an old thing," I said. "I threw it out. My mom must have brought it back in from the garbage can. She likes that old thing."

Tony slammed me in the elbow with the bear's head. The bear didn't look too happy about it.

I handed Tony some darts, hoping to get his

mind off the bear. He was tossing it in the air like a ball, higher and higher. The last time he tossed it, he forgot to catch it. It fell hard on the floor. I wanted to pick it up and dust it off right away, but I felt Tony looking at me. So I just opened up my closet door and put the bear inside. Then I closed the door behind me and began playing darts.

Later, when Tony left, I took the bear out from the closet and set him back on my bureau. It seemed the right thing to do. I felt we were waiting for Grandmom together.

5

Grandmom was in trouble. She had given her ankle a bad sprain and the doctor told her to stay off it as much as possible. The doctor wanted her to stay in her bedroom for a couple of days. Then she could use a cane to get around the bottom floor of the house.

"Under no circumstances can you go out," my mom reminded her when they got home.

Mom let Grandmom use the guest bedroom on the main floor near the kitchen, because she couldn't climb steps. She bought Grandmom Sarah a big bag of colored wool and two new books from the bookstore. "This should keep you busy for a while," my mom said as we pulled Grandmom's favorite rocking chair into the bedroom. When I was sick with a sore throat or an upset stomach, Mom usually bought me a model car or a comic book.

It was on the fourth day that Grandmom called me into her room. She was standing near the open window, leaning on her cane. Grandmom always kept a window slightly open in her bedroom. "I like to smell that ocean air," she'd say.

She had something else to say today. "Allan, you've got to do me a favor. I thought this ankle would be healed in no time, but I can see it's going to take some more time. And even then, I'm going to have to be careful walking outside until the weather gets warmer."

She sat down on the edge of the bed and she was whispering as if she didn't want anyone else to hear her.

"You've got to go to Silver Lake and feed the ducks," she said. "I haven't been there all week and I know they're waiting for me."

"Grandmom. Lots of people feed the ducks in the winter," I told her. "I bet they won't even know you're not there."

That was definitely not the right thing to say. Grandmom's face tightened and her glare just about knocked me off the bed. Even her voice got stronger as she stood up, leaning on her cane. "They absolutely *positively* will know I'm not there," she said. "You can't depend on anyone else when it comes to something like this. If everyone thought that way, that it was someone else's job, no one would show up. I'm especially worried about Snowbird. She's very picky about her food and she can't fly very far. She's really stuck on

Silver Lake and dependent on what we feed her. I usually keep her company while she eats. What about it, Allan? Are we sticking together on this one? I want Snowbird fed."

I thought it strange that she singled out the little white duck, and wondered if she was sending me a message. There wasn't much else I could do but say yes. I just hoped that Grandmom's ankle would heal fast so that she'd be back doing her job again.

It wasn't easy, the first time I went back to Silver Lake. I had almost forgotten about Snowbird and everything else that had happened there, but now, watching the ducks sitting on the ice like little statues, it all came back to me. Grandmom was right about one thing. They needed food. The lake wasn't defrosting and the ducks were squatting there, in the middle of it, looking very unhappy. Even Big Al and Evelyn weren't too active. They were resting on a hill nearby, with Snowbird in between them, as if they were all keeping each other company.

I stood there for a moment and then opened the bag Grandmom had given me. It was the strangest thing, what happened next. It was as if everyone were waiting for me, as if they knew exactly what I was there for. First, the sea gulls flew overhead making loud cawing sounds as if they were sending out a message that dinner was being served. A few of the ducks hobbled toward me over the ice. Some more hurried toward me from under the bridge. And some even came out of the green house. The birds were still flying overhead and suddenly there was an awful lot of noise and flapping of wings. *Caw, caw, quack, quack.* There was plenty of conversation going on, as if the birds were telling each other that food was coming.

I threw the corn seed onto the dirt around me and some onto the ice. It made me feel good to watch the birds hurry toward it and gobble it up. Evelyn and Big Al must have been hungry because they came very close to me, almost right up to my feet.

But it was Snowbird that I really noticed. Because she was smaller than the others she was getting pushed around. I sure knew that feeling. Every time she went to peck at some food, a larger bird would swoop down and push it aside. Well, I couldn't let that happen. I tossed an extra big pile of corn seed near Snowbird, but every time I bent down to push it closer to her, she moved away as if she was afraid of me. I wanted to tell her not to be afraid, that I would rather lose every model car in my collection than hurt her one bit. Because no one was around, I could talk without worrying about anyone else hearing. It was easier that way to apologize to Snowbird, and I promised

I would never again throw one stone, not one small pebble into the lake or at any bird living there or anywhere else.

But Snowbird didn't eat that day.

Or the next day when I went back. By the third day, it was all that I had on my mind at school. I couldn't wait until the bell rang so I could run over to Silver Lake with the corn seed and try again to get Snowbird to eat.

"Where are you going?" Flute asked as he caught up with me by the front door of the school.

"To Silver Lake," I told him. "I have to feed the ducks for my grandmom."

"I'll come with you," Flute said. "I used to feed them all the time, but now I have flute lessons and I have to practice a lot."

When we got to the lake, the green-necked mallards were lined up in a row, as if they were stuck to the ice. There were some new ducks there. They had black heads and a white stripe down their necks.

"They're the Canadian geese," Flute said. "They stop in on their way home. Every year about twenty of them come and eat. Sometimes I think they come to visit and catch up with the news."

I felt comfortable being at the lake with Flute. He seemed to like feeding the ducks as much as I did. He took some of the corn seed and threw

53

it in the water while I stayed on the slope surrounding the lake, feeding the birds there. Snowbird stayed off to the side with Big Al and Evelyn while the other birds ate, but when most of them left to go back onto the ice, she waddled over with the geese and began to peck away at the corn seed. She kept coming closer and closer to me until she was right near my shoe.

"You can trust me," I whispered to her. "I'm your friend, honest. Grandmom and I will see to it that you never go hungry. As long as I live at Three-Hundred Park Place Avenue, I promise you that." Anyone in Mapletown would agree that I never ever broke a promise. I told Snowbird that before Flute came back.

"I've got to get going," he said. "I've got a flute lesson in a half hour." He looked at his watch. Flute was always looking at his watch. I never wore one.

"I'll come with you tomorrow to feed them," he said before he left.

That was the trouble with Flute. He always expected to do something with me again, just because we did it once. I mean, I did things twice with friends, but Flute didn't understand that I was working hard to be part of Tony and Pete's group of friends. Everyone wanted to be friends with them. Tony didn't let just *anyone* into that group. The last thing I needed was to be thought of as part of the bandies. No one in Tony and Pete's group had *bandies* as friends. Of course I didn't tell Flute any of this because I didn't want to hurt his feelings. Flute seemed pretty sensitive about things. I once saw his eyes fill up when we saw a movie in school about dead sea gulls caught in an oil slick that had washed up on shore. I was afraid he was going to cry right there in his seat that afternoon.

Tony, Pete, and I went bicycle riding one day after school. We rode the whole length of the boardwalk, which was six miles up and six miles back. I had ridden my bicycle all around Maple-town, but I never pedaled for so long at one time. Tony and Pete were used to it.

"I've got to stop and rest," I told Tony before we were ready to ride back home.

Tony looked as if he didn't believe me. "You tired already?" he asked.

Well, I tried not to take too long resting against the boardwalk railing, while Tony and Pete rode around in circles on the boardwalk. It was a clear day, and though it was cold, the sky was deep blue and the ocean was the same color. But even after the ride, as tired as I was, I had to go over to the Lake and feed the ducks because each night I had to report in to Grandmom.

"Did you throw the seed onto the ice the way I told you?"

"Yes, Grandmom, I did."

"Did you leave some on the grass so they could graze a bit?"

"Yes, I did."

"Did you make sure Snowbird ate?"

"She sure did, Grandmom."

"Tomorrow, I'll give you some money to get another bag of corn seed from the pet shop on Main Street," she said. "And maybe some little fish, too."

"Sure, Grandmom."

"Good. Good," she'd say at the end of each day. "I'm proud of you, Allan. I knew you wouldn't let me down."

I wanted to tell Grandmom it wasn't easy walking over to that lake after riding twelve miles on my bicycle. My legs felt wobbly all the way. But I felt sorry for Grandmom Sarah and, if my feeding the ducks made her a little happier, I was willing to do it. She was spending so much time alone. My parents were at work during the day and I was at school. I was usually the first to get home and Grandmom was usually waiting for me in the kitchen when I got there. She was able to walk a few feet now with a cane.

"How was school today, Allan?" she'd ask.

"Okay," I'd answer. I wasn't as good at telling stories as she was.

Then we'd have milk and cookies. Grandmom sometimes ate even more cookies than I did.

"It's sure a long day," she'd say sometimes. "I can hear that clock ticking in the hall, just about every minute."

I knew what she meant. I listened to the clock ticking in school a lot. I'd think about the clock ticking at the school in Mapletown. It didn't seem to tick so slow there.

By the second week, I was beginning to look forward to seeing Evelyn and Al and Snowbird each day. And I felt they were beginning to look forward to seeing me. Sometimes I was a block away, just walking toward them, and they'd know I was coming. I don't know how they knew, but they did. I'd hear the *caws* and the *quacks* and Evelyn and Al honking even before they could see me. Snowbird was usually with them and Evelyn and Al looked as if they didn't mind that at all. The three of them were walking together as if they were old friends. I could see the other ducks flying around in circles from one end of the lake to the other, getting all excited as I carried the bag of corn seed toward them.

One afternoon as I stood there scattering the corn seed up and down the side of the lake, I heard a familiar voice behind me. "Look who's feeding

the ducks," Tony said. Pete, of course, was with
him.

Tony started laughing. It was the same laugh
that he used when he saw the stuffed bear in my
room. I didn't like it then and I still didn't like it.
Before I could stop him, he grabbed the bag of
corn seed and shook it all in the air, emptying it
out. The seed scattered around, scaring the ducks.
A few of them flew off into the air. Evelyn and
Al looked up at him, disgusted. Snowbird hurried
off, leaving her dinner on the ground. But Tony
wasn't satisfied with just scaring them. I saw him
looking through the grass, then on the side of the
hill, and I knew what he was looking for. At last
he found some small stones.

He threw one into the lake. Most of the ice had
melted, and the stone made a ring, a circle that
got bigger and bigger. The ducks that were left
scattered, even Evelyn and Al and Snowbird.

"How do you like that?" Tony asked. "Even
those geese are running." He and Pete picked up
some more pebbles and began to throw them.

I knew I couldn't stand there anymore and let
them do it. I knew the next stone might hit a
bull's-eye and if I stood there and let it happen,
it would be just as much my fault as if I had thrown
it myself. My throat got awfully dry and I had a
cramp in my stomach when I walked over to Tony
and pulled back the hand that held the stones.

"Don't throw any more," I said.

"Let go of my hand," Tony ordered.

"I'll let go if you tell me you won't throw any more," I said back. Big Al and Evelyn and Snowbird were looking over at us as if they knew something important was going on.

There was a lot of pushing and shoving after that, but finally Tony gave an extra shove and I wound up in the lake, in water up to my knees.

That night when Grandmom called me into her bedroom to get her nightly report about the news from Silver Lake, I left out some parts. I didn't want to lie to Grandmom, but her foot was still troubling her and I didn't want to make it worse by telling her about Tony and Pete and the rock throwing. So I told Grandmom everything was just fine and then I spent the rest of the night staring up at the ceiling, unable to sleep.

6

Things were about as bad as they could get that week. I never thought I'd have this kind of problem in school. At lunch in the cafeteria, I stood there with a tray in my hands wondering which table I should sit at. Flute was waving toward me. He was sitting with the bandies and looked as if he expected me to come and sit down with them. Tony was waving to me, too. I was sort of surprised about that, even though I usually ate lunch at his table with his friends. After he threw me in the lake, I didn't expect him to be so friendly, but that was the way Tony was. He forgot real quick about things. Sometimes that was good, like now.

I walked slowly down the aisle toward Flute.

"Hey, Allan. I want you to meet some of my friends," Flute said. "Joey, Frank, Bob. This is my friend, Allan. He's the one who taught me how to make all those model cars."

I smiled at everyone while I leaned my tray

against the table. I was really hungry, so I started munching on my French fries. There was an empty seat next to Flute and I thought he expected me to sit in it. I ate up all my French fries standing there deciding what to do.

"You coming over after school to finish the car?" I asked Flute.

"Sure am," he answered.

"Okay," I said. "I'll see you then." I thought that was a pretty good time to take my tray and head toward Tony's table, even though I wouldn't have minded eating lunch at Flute's table. I just knew Tony wouldn't like it if I did.

"I thought you were going to eat lunch with the bandies today," Tony said as I sat down in a chair at the end of the table.

"Are you kidding?" I answered. "He just keeps bothering me about those model cars."

I ate the meat loaf quickly and dumped out the gravy and the roll. I just wanted the lunch hour to be over as fast as possible so I could get out of there.

When I got home, Grandmom met me at the front door. She didn't even wait for me to take off my hat and jacket and get some cookies.

"You've got to get over to the lake right away," she said. "It's freezing out today and those little babies will need food."

I wasn't too anxious to run into Tony there, so

I hurried to the lake and didn't stay very long.

"You'd better just stay out of Tony's way," I told Evelyn and Al and Snowbird, who was standing in the middle between the two geese. "I just can't be around all the time." I scattered the corn seed as far as I could and watched the birds munching on it. I noticed when Evelyn and Al and Snowbird were finished eating, they walked away together, almost as if they were a family.

The freezing weather was also bothering my parents. The bungalow in back that we could rent out in the summer should have had the water drained out of the pipes from the main house, but Mom and Dad hadn't known about it, until it was too late. The pipes burst and a plumber had to come in to fix everything.

"This old house," my mom said, and the way she said it I knew she was wishing she were back in Mapletown also.

So that Saturday I decided to go back to our old house, which wasn't really old at all, just twelve years old compared to this eighty-two-year-old house. I took some money from the penny jar I kept on the floor and told my mom I was going bowling. I didn't like telling her a lie, but Mapletown was one and a half hours away by bus, and I knew she wouldn't like me taking such a long ride by myself. It wasn't a trip I wanted to make with someone else. I knew I had to go back alone. The bus stop was just five blocks down Main Street.

All the way to Mapletown, I had this real excited feeling in my stomach. I kept thinking about David and my house and all the things I hadn't seen in over six months. When the bus stopped in Mapletown, I just about ran off it. It was a ten-block walk to my old neighborhood, but I didn't mind. I liked looking in the store windows, the bakery shop where I used to get my doughnuts on the way from school, the barbershop where I went for my haircuts. I peeked in the window next to the striped barbershop pole. Sol, the barber, saw me. He waved and gave me a big smile, as if I still lived on Sandy Hill Road.

During the ten-block walk, that's just what I pretended. That it was a Saturday and I was coming back from my haircut and that I still lived on Sandy Hill Road and David was waiting to play with me. When I turned the corner on my old block, I really felt I was still living in the house next to David. My stomach just about rolled over as I walked toward it.

Some things had changed. I hadn't expected that. I had left my house white, with redwood on the top half of the house. Someone had painted the white, blue, and there was no redwood anymore. It was just a big blue house. All the rosebushes were gone and in their place was a rock garden. The new people had put awnings over the top bedroom windows, white ones. I didn't like them. Mom always said awnings would take away the sun from the bedrooms. I guessed it was dark now upstairs.

The strangest thing happened as I stood there. I felt as if I should go inside. I knew I didn't live there anymore, at least my mind knew it, but my body kept wanting to walk right up to the front door, run up the stairs, and flop on the bed in my room. It would always be my room, I thought, as I stood there. I didn't care how many people bought that house or lived in it. It would always be *my* bedroom, and a part of me would always live there.

There was no car in the driveway or in front of the house. The shades were down as if no one were home. I walked up the driveway toward the backyard. I couldn't believe my eyes when I got there. All the grass was gone. So was the swing set I used to use when I was a kid. And the rubber tire tied to the tree where I used to swing was gone. The whole backyard was covered with cement and in the center of the yard was a pool. A real pool, not as big as the one on the boardwalk in Ocean View, but big enough for a couple of people to swim around. There were beach chairs all around it, the wooden kind that you didn't have to take inside in the winter. There was no water in the pool. It had a cover over it.

I looked up toward the top floor at my bedroom window. I always used to look down into the backyard, first thing in the morning when I got up. I wanted to do that right now, be up there looking down at everything, waiting for David or one of my other friends to knock at my front door so we could walk to school together, or run up to the shopping center.

Thinking of David made me want to see him right away. I ran across the street to his house and knocked on the door. David's mother answered. She was wearing her typing clothes, a fresh white blouse and a skirt. She did work for a doctor, typing all his reports in her house. She always told David and me she got dressed to work just as if she were going into the office. I knew David's mother hadn't changed and that made me feel good. I also smelled something real good in the kitchen and remembered Saturday was Mrs. Butler's baking day.

"Allan! I don't believe it!" She looked behind me as if she were expecting to see someone. "Aren't your parents with you?" she asked.

I shook my head. "They were busy," I told her. "I decided to come alone."

The smile on Mrs. Butler's face turned into a frown. She patted my head softly. "Come in," she said. "I just finished making some chocolate chip cookies. You know I always make them on Saturday. I bet that's why you came today." She was smiling again.

I let Mrs. Butler lead me into the kitchen. "Is David home?" I asked.

"No," she answered. "He slept over at Jimmy's house last night, and he isn't home yet."

"Jimmy Burns?" I asked.

"Yes, that's the boy," David's mother answered.

"I didn't know he was Jimmy's friend," I said.

Mrs. Butler placed a plate of cookies on the table in front of me and then poured me a glass of milk. "Well Allan, you know, after you left, David was so lonely," she said, sitting down next to me at the table. "He must have moped around here for weeks. Then he just had to make some new friends. Know what I mean?"

"Sure," I answered. But I wasn't too happy about Jimmy Burns.

I guess it showed on my face. Mrs. Butler squeezed my hand. "If you had just called him, I know he would have stayed home to see you. He's missed you so much."

I sat there for a while while Mrs. Butler put some more cookies on my plate.

"Do you think David will be home soon?" I asked.

Mrs. Butler looked at the clock. "They were going bowling this afternoon."

"Maybe I'll go to the alley and meet him." I started to get up but Mrs. Butler's hand was on my shoulder. I sat back down in the seat again.

"I'm going to call your parents, Allan. I would want them to call me if David were at your house. They'll want to know you got here safely."

"But they don't even know I'm here," I said without thinking.

"Then they should," David's mother answered and she had the same look on her face my mother got when she had made up her mind to do something. She dialed my home.

"Hi, Betty," she said. "Yes, it's Etta. I'm fine. Just fine. I've been wanting to call you, but today, I had a special reason. Allan has paid us a visit."

Well, I didn't know what was going on at the other end of the telephone conversation, but I guessed my mother wasn't too happy about the news. There were a lot of "okays" from Mrs. Butler's end, and "of courses," and finally Mrs. Butler said, "I'll see you later."

"Your parents are going to pick you up," she said. "They don't want you to take that long trip back by yourself."

Mrs. Butler tried Jimmy's house while we were waiting for my parents. It seemed after bowling,

Jimmy's father had driven them to a movie. I couldn't believe it. David and I never went to a movie after bowling. We usually got some French fries at the restaurant next door and sat in a booth for as long as they'd let us, dipping the fries into ketchup.

After a little while my mom and dad showed up. They sat for a while with Etta Butler, and had some cake and tea. They talked about the new house, which was really the eighty-two-year-old house, and the old house that wasn't ours anymore. They looked across the street toward it and I saw my mom's eyes fill up the way they did before she cried. There was a lot of kissing and hugging before we left, but in the car, no one said anything. My dad and mom didn't talk to each other, and they didn't say one word to me. I was beginning to wonder if they knew I was in the backseat.

"Go to your room, Allan," my dad said when we got home. "I'll be up there in a few minutes."

It seemed like hours even though the clock only said five minutes had passed when I heard my dad's footsteps coming up toward my bedroom.

"You know you should have told us you wanted to visit our old neighborhood," my dad said, sitting on the edge of the bed. "We would have driven you. You're not old enough to take a long trip like that by yourself."

"I didn't think you'd take the time," I told my dad. "I know you've been busy with your new job."

"Not too busy for this," Dad answered. "You said you were going bowling, Allan, and you lied to your mother."

I felt uncomfortable about that, as if I were wearing a shoe that didn't fit.

"We're going to have to ground you. Two weeks, no going out on weekends or after school, and nobody coming over."

Grandmom didn't make it any easier for me when I came home after school during my grounding time. Even though her leg was better and she was practicing walking around the house, she still couldn't go outside.

"Now who's going to feed the ducks?" she asked when she heard I was grounded. Other than saying that, she wasn't talking to me much. She didn't ask me to unknot her wool. She didn't even remind me any more about Snowbird.

But she didn't have to. Each time I looked outside, I'd remember the little white duck that was the color of the snow-filled sky. I wondered if she knew her mate wasn't coming back, or if she was waiting for him, like I was waiting to feel as happy as I used to feel when I lived in Mapletown. I wondered if she felt trapped living on Silver Lake the way I felt living in Ocean View.

7

It was the greatest way to be ungrounded, I thought. Dad and I were going to go to the bay to go fishing off the pier.

"Now just be careful," Mom said before we left. "Don't go sitting on the edge of the dock. You could fall in. And be careful when you cast that you don't hook anyone."

Mom was that kind of person. She always had a list of things to remember and remind me about. Sometimes I think she sat up all night worrying about what was going to happen tomorrow.

"I don't know why you didn't ask Flute to come," my mom said, handing me my fishing rod from the downstairs closet.

"Or even Tony," my dad said as he put on his fishing jacket with all the special pockets in it. "I told him he could take whomever he wanted."

I didn't tell my dad, but I really felt like being alone with him. Besides, I had to think every day now about who I was sitting with at lunch. Yesterday Flute had walked through the lunch line with me, and when we got out he stood there as if he were waiting for me to sit down at his table. But I always saw Tony's face somewhere in the back of the lunch room, watching us. It wasn't just deciding whether or not to sit with Flute that bothered me. I knew it was like walking over a big line, and if I sat with the bandies, I might never be able to cross back over again to be with Tony. It just didn't work that way.

The sunrise that morning was the best I had seen yet. It looked as if someone had taken a paintbrush and made big long strokes across the sky in pink and light blue and even little bits of yellow. The sea gulls were circling overhead when we reached the bay.

Dad parked the car in the parking lot facing the bay. We got all our equipment out of the trunk of his car and took a spot along the railing at the edge of the dock. Dad and I used worms for bait. I didn't much like putting them at the end of the hook, but that was part of fishing and if you wanted to be a real fisherman, you had to do the dirty work, too.

"Isn't this the best?" Dad said, looking out over the sky. It was real quiet on the bay and all the shades in the houses looking out over us were still down. But we weren't the only ones awake. The big fishing boats were already going out and there were other fishermen on the dock, casting their lines. We all had to be very careful not to tangle our lines together.

"Get anything?" my dad asked a few of the fishermen who had big white buckets beside them.

"Few trout," one man answered.

I looked inside. The fish in the bucket didn't look too excited about being there. They weren't moving around at all.

We sat there for a long time watching our fishing lines dipping into the water. That was the nice thing about fishing. I really didn't care how many fish I caught. There was just a nice quietness about things and no rush. No one seemed to be watching a clock at the pier. You could get real dirty and smelly and no one cared.

It was fun fishing with Dad. He got hungry all the time and there was a snack bar right off the pier.

"How about some French fries?" he asked. So we went and got some.

"How about some soda?" he said later, so we went and got some Cokes.

"Maybe it's time for some sandwiches," he said in a few hours, while our white buckets were still empty.

We had been there about four hours, talking to the other fishermen and looking in a lot of buckets, when my line started bending down toward the water. I ran over to it and tried to pull it back, but it was too heavy. Dad helped me while the other fishermen around put their poles down to watch. I felt real important there, pulling on that line, reeling the fish in, until I found out I didn't have a fish at all. I had the biggest clump of seaweed I'd ever seen.

Everyone around me had a good laugh over that but me. That's why, when the line bent again a couple of minutes later, I didn't pay much attention. This time I didn't rush so much and instead of calling my dad, I just pulled and tugged with all my might, expecting to see more seaweed at the end of my line. I guess my face must have been getting pretty red because that seaweed was giving me quite a time getting it up.

Was I surprised when a fish wiggling every which way came up instead! It was giving me a real fight. Dad jumped up but by that time I had gotten it over the side of the rail and it was flapping on the dock.

"Allan, that's a big one," Dad said. "You pulled it in all by yourself. It must be at least three pounds."

I couldn't believe all the fuss that was made about that fish. The fishermen who were laughing before weren't laughing now. They were standing around me, taking turns picking up the fish and looking at it.

"That's some catch," one man said. "You should take that boy out on a boat some day. He's a natural fisherman."

Well, I didn't much agree about that. I didn't know what I was doing to catch that fish. It just came along and caught itself.

One of the fishermen showed me how to skin the fish and take the bones out. I didn't really like to do it but he explained that that was part of fishing and tonight when we ate the fish, we'd see how great it could taste.

I couldn't wait to tell someone about the big fish I caught. It was a story I had to share right away because I was so excited about it. I wanted to tell someone what it was like to pull that fish up while it was fighting on the other end of the line, and to have so many people say such great things about me. As soon as I got home — after my mother made a fuss and put some eggs and bread crumbs on the fish and set it in the refrigerator — I called Tony.

"You should have seen the fish I caught," I said. "My dad said it was at least three pounds. He couldn't believe I pulled it up all by myself."

"I go fishing all the time," Tony answered. "My dad takes me out on the big fishing boats. We stay out all day sometimes."

There didn't seem to be much to say after that. I thought of calling Flute, but I didn't. Then he'd really think I was his friend. Instead I decided to call David. I took some money from my coin jar on the floor and ran up to the boardwalk.

"Hi, Mrs. Butler," I said when David's mother answered. "Is David home?"

"No, he's bowling," his mother answered.

"Bowling? On Sunday afternoon?" I said.

"Yes. He's joined a bowling league."

"Is that so," I said. I thought David hated leagues. He once said he didn't want to have to show up at a certain time on a certain day and play with certain people. He once said that.

"How about if I have him call you when he gets in," Mrs. Butler said.

"Sure, that would be great," I told her. "I caught a three-pound fish," I added.

"Imagine that," David's mother's voice got louder. "I bet you're going to eat it for dinner tonight."

"Sure am," I answered.

When I hung up, I stood there for a minute looking out over the ocean from the phone booth. It was funny about living here. You could look down any street and see the ocean. It was always there, like a big wall, and you couldn't go past it. No matter how many miles down you went, the ocean always stared back at you. Today a thick fog was coming in, covering the water and even the boardwalk. The fog horn was blowing every minute, to warn the boats to come in before they got stuck out there.

Today the ocean was making all kinds of sounds and noises and thrashing about. There weren't many people on the boardwalk and the ones that were there, I didn't know. I didn't feel like going back home yet and I didn't feel like going to Tony's and hearing about his big fishing trips, and I didn't feel like calling Flute and feeling guilty about it because I knew what Tony thought about Flute and everyone else in the band. I didn't feel like talking to Grandmom Sarah because she wasn't in too good a mood lately. "I've got to get out of this house," she kept saying. Each time, she said it as if she'd never said it before, even though she said it just about every hour.

So I decided to walk by Silver Lake and say hello to the ducks. I didn't have any food with me but I thought they might like to see me anyway. Maybe they missed me during the two weeks I couldn't go out after school. Maybe they'd be interested in my fish story since they were always trying to catch fish themselves. I walked slowly along the brown grass on the side of the lake. There weren't many ducks around today. There were a few green-necked mallards and some sea gulls flying overhead. I kept thinking the rest of the ducks would be further down on the other side of the bridge, but as I walked toward home and passed the bridge, I didn't see any of the ducks I expected to see.

In fact, I didn't see Snowbird, or Evelyn and Al, not even under the willow tree. At first I thought maybe they were in the green house by the lake so I peeked in, but there was no one there. Then I thought maybe I missed them when I was walking, so I walked over the bridge, to the other side of the lake, into the town of Sea Bright, and all the way back again. I did that twice, walking clear around the lake, watching everything that moved. But there was no white duck, not even near the little house where she usually hung out, and there were no geese honking anywhere around. I guess I should have been glad, because if Snowbird had left to find another home at a nearby pond, I wouldn't have to worry about her anymore. But it felt strange, standing there, not hearing the geese honking, not seeing little Snowbird going about her day.

As soon as I got home, I told Grandmom. She just snapped back at me, "Well, I don't blame them one bit if they went off to some other place. The lake is filled with garbage, and people don't give them the respect they deserve. You'd think someone would protect them by putting up a sign telling anyone who dared throw anything at them that there would be a fine, you would think that, wouldn't you?"

I didn't know if she was *asking* me that question or not, but she sure was mad about it. "When I get out of this house, I just might do something about it myself," Grandmom said.

I hoped Grandmom would. Maybe that's why Snowbird and the geese left. Maybe they thought I would help them out. Maybe they expected that of me. Maybe they thought I was their friend because I fed them every day and talked to them, and maybe they just got disgusted one day because no one seemed to care.

The next morning when I got up, I listened very carefully at my window. I could usually hear Evelyn and Al honking very early, but I didn't hear them saying a thing. That afternoon when I ran to the lake after school with some corn seed, I fed all the birds but Evelyn and Al and Snowbird. They weren't there, and I didn't know if they ever would be again. I don't know why, but I felt I had let them down. And now it was too late to tell them I was sorry.

8

When I wrote the composition yesterday about Snowbird and the ducks on Silver Lake, I didn't expect the teacher to ask me to read it out loud. I just wrote about what was on my mind, and the ducks and the block party coming up today were all I could think about.

"Allen," Mrs. Barber called out my name at the beginning of the class. "I was very impressed with your composition. I would like you to read it to the class."

I didn't like to get up in front of the class, and I especially didn't like to read aloud, but when Mrs. Barber asked you to do something, she didn't expect *no* for an answer.

I was glad Tony and Pete weren't in my English class, and neither was Flute. I went to the front of the class and began reading my composition, although my handwriting wasn't too clear, even for me.

"I didn't know what I was doing on Silver Lake,

but I knew I was a little white duck. I didn't know what my mom and dad and grandmom Sarah were doing there either, or why they looked like little white ducks also.

"We were all paddling around as if we belonged there with the other ducks, as if we spent every day there, just swimming around.

"All of a sudden my grandmom Sarah called, 'You must come with me and see the block party.' She was heading toward the bridge. We followed Grandmom under the bridge, and sure enough, as we got closer, we heard music and people laughing and lots of noise. At first, all I saw was some tents and a lot of people walking around them.

" 'What fun everyone is having,' Dad said.

" 'They look like such nice people.' My mom went closer so she could get a better look. I went with her.

"While we were watching, some boys about my age left the block party and came over to the edge of the lake. I thought maybe they were going to throw us some popcorn. Grandmom Sarah did, too. She started flapping her wings.

'Look at the ducks,' one of them yelled.

"Then he picked up something from the ground and tossed it into the water.

" 'Let's get out of here,' Dad yelled. 'He's throwing stones. Come on, follow me, everyone.'

" 'Hey, look at the ducks run away,' one of the

boys yelled. Now they were running, too, and I was getting pretty scared. Even though we were swimming fast, the stones they were throwing were getting close. One almost hit me in the wing. Finally, they stopped following us.

"As soon as we got back to the little green house where we stayed when the weather got bad, Dad called a family meeting. He only called family meetings when there was big trouble.

" 'We're going to have to leave here,' he said. 'We just can't stay here anymore. We don't know when those boys will come back. Next time we might not be so lucky.'

"I didn't want to go anywhere. I liked living on this lake. I couldn't imagine living somewhere else, not having Ocean View on one side and Sea Bright on the other. I couldn't imagine not seeing the same people every morning feeding us from the bridge, or from their cars.

"The next day we flew to another lake nearby. But it wasn't the same. And I knew that we would have to leave if those boys ever found us again. I really don't know why they would want to hurt us, because we would never hurt them that way."

I didn't even look up after I finished reading. I just sat down quickly in my chair. I didn't think anyone in the class liked my story because no one applauded.

"We could all learn a lesson from Allan's composition," Mrs. Barber said. "You have an A on that, Allan."

I felt happy about the A, but not too happy about everyone in the class knowing what I was thinking. To make myself feel better, I walked over the bridge after school, toward the block party in Sea Bright. I didn't have to rush home. My parents were going out to dinner with the people from Dad's pharmacy. He was all excited. "I think they really are getting used to me," he told Grandmom. Then he asked her if she would mind making me dinner.

I could hear the music even as I walked and by the time I got to Main Street, I forgot about everything that was bothering me. Four blocks of Main Street were all roped off so that automobiles couldn't drive down them. There was a little band playing in the middle of the street, and a lot of people were dancing with each other. A clown was giving out balloons and just about everybody was carrying one.

Mapletown had a Main Street, but it was much different from Sea Bright's. Mapletown had plenty of stores and gas stations. But in Sea Bright, the streets were lined with big trees and there were benches to sit on in front of every store.

Everybody at the block party seemed to be buying something. Some people were buying furniture and carrying it off in station wagons. Others were carrying chairs and lamps. I was interested in playing the games, especially the balloon game that was set up on the corner. I gave the man behind the counter twenty-five cents.

The balloons were filled with water, and all I had to do was throw the dart and break the balloon. I had three chances. From where I was standing, it looked pretty easy to do.

I threw one dart and missed. I threw the second dart and missed. I couldn't understand how I was missing when I aimed that dart right at the yellow balloon. I didn't feel too bad though, because someone was standing next to me throwing her darts and she was missing, too. My third dart got stuck in the wall behind the balloons.

"That wasn't as easy as I thought it would be," said the girl standing next to me.

She looked familiar and then I remembered where I had seen her. She played the horn in the same band as Flute. I stood there watching her throw the rest of her darts, missing all the balloons.

"I really liked that composition you wrote," she said as she paid the man another quarter. "I sit in the back of the room in your English class. My name's Beth."

Beth had long, silver-blonde hair that kept falling down in her eyes every time she threw a dart. I didn't think she was going to get too far like that. She hit everything but the balloons. I couldn't help laughing when one of the darts landed in the tree behind the large board holding the balloons.

"I wanted to win that little white teddy bear," she said as she looked down at her last quarter. She didn't look too happy about losing her money.

I had one dollar left from my allowance. I gave the man another quarter. Beth stood next to me watching me throw the darts.

I guess I was thinking about the little white bear and how Beth looked while she was staring at it. I aimed real carefully while I spent one quarter and then another. I was on my last quarter when I finally busted a balloon.

"You have the choice of a model car, a bag of marbles, or the little white bear," the man said.

I wouldn't have minded getting the car. It was small, but bright red, and it might have looked good in my collection. If Beth weren't standing next to me, it would have been easy to choose. But I knew how she was feeling about that bear.

"I'll take the bear," I said.

I plopped it in her hands and watched her eyes get real wide. "You're giving me the bear?" she shouted.

I wished she hadn't said it so loud because a lot

of people turned around and the man behind the counter smiled. "I've got enough cars and marbles," I told her.

She was petting the bear and holding it real tight. "You want to get some cotton candy?" she asked.

"I don't have any money left," I told her, digging into my pockets.

"I have a quarter." Beth pulled it out of her pocket. "We could share it," she said.

So we walked to the corner where a man stood pulling cotton candy from a machine and putting it on a stick. We ate the cotton candy real fast. I noticed she gave me more than half. Finally the music stopped and the people started putting their things away. It was later than I thought, much later than dinnertime.

"I'd better get home," I said.

"Me, too." Beth was still holding tight to the bear. "Thanks for the bear." She waved good-bye as she ran down the sidewalk.

I started running, too. It was nearly seven o'clock and dark out. I couldn't believe time had passed so quickly. I decided to cut across the park near the lake. You can imagine my surprise when I saw Grandmom Sarah standing in the center of the street in between two lines of cars. They were all honking their horns and their front lights splashed across the street.

I ran real fast toward her, and then as I got closer, I saw Big Al and Evelyn and Snowbird. They were back.

"What's wrong, Grandmom?" I asked. "What are you doing out here?" The doctor had said Grandmom could take short walks in front of the house with a cane, but this was no short walk.

"I got worried about you, Allan," Grandmom said. "I thought maybe you were here feeding the ducks." The horns were still honking but Grandmom didn't seem to care. "And then I found them. Big Al and Evelyn and Snowbird just standing here in the middle of the street."

Well, the lines of cars kept getting longer and traffic was backed up as far as I could see. Grandmom talked real fast, giving me instructions. "Run back to the house, Allan, and get the bag of corn seed on the steps going down to the basement. Hurry now. And watch yourself crossing the streets."

It didn't take me long to do what Grandmom asked. When I got back, there were a lot of angry drivers yelling out their open car windows. A few even stood where Grandmom was, trying to get Evelyn and Big Al and Snowbird to move. But every time the drivers got near them, the geese would make a lot of loud noises and spread their wings real wide, as if they were getting ready to chase everyone off the street.

"Now open the bag and make a thin trail behind us," Grandmom told me as she held onto my arm with one hand and leaned on her cane with the other.

As we walked across the street toward the lake, the geese and Snowbird followed us, eating the seed as they went. We got them out of the way of traffic and near the edge of the lake. When they were done eating, they slid into the water and cleaned their feathers while the cars that had been waiting passed by. I noticed a lot of people were smiling now and waving to us.

We walked home very slowly. I could tell Grandmom was getting tired. "I guess I did a little too much today," she said as she sat down on a bench to rest. I sat down with her.

"I'm worried, Allan," she said, putting her arm around me. "I don't know how those birds are going to survive. It's odd, how everyone likes to watch the ducks and sometimes they feed them, but I don't think they really care about what happens to them. There's more traffic than ever around here and people seem to have forgotten that the ducks have their home on Silver Lake."

"We care about them, Grandmom," I said.

"Yes, you're right, Allan, we do. I guess if we

care, we have to do something to see that the birds on this lake are protected."

I wasn't sure what she was thinking, but Grandmom Sarah got right up from the bench. She didn't seem tired anymore.

9

I was beginning to wonder where Flute was when he called me one morning on the telephone. He had been out of school for two days.

"Hey, Allan, could you bring home my homework today? I have a real bad sore throat."

"Sure, Flute," I said. "I hope you feel better."

Every day for a week, I went to Flute's house before I went home. Flute lived about eight blocks away from me but I didn't mind the walk.

I had never been to Flute's house before. He had asked me to come over but I couldn't see myself telling Tony I had been to Flute's house, and Tony had a way of finding out everything that went on in school and after it. But I thought bringing homework was more a job than a visit.

On the third day Mrs. Greenwood let me go up to Flute's room to visit with him.

"Just stay near the doorway, Allan," she said. "I don't want you to catch his cold."

When I walked into the room, I felt I was standing right in the middle of the ocean. Flute's house was across the street from the boardwalk and beside Flute's bed was a large picture window. When I stood in front of it, I could see the beach.

"Boy, what a neat thing to look at every day," I told Flute.

The window was open a little bit and I could even hear the waves thrashing about much clearer than I heard them at home.

I guess I didn't exactly listen to Flute's mother about where I should stand because before I knew it, I was standing by the open window, just looking out at the ocean and the waves. There were a lot of whitecaps today. Even though the sun was out and it didn't look like it was going to rain anywhere around, there was probably a storm at sea that hadn't come in yet.

"I think it's the best thing, living by the ocean," Flute said. He looked very serious even though his nose was red from blowing it. "My dad always says once you live near the water, you can never live away from it."

I met Flute's dad on the fourth day that I delivered Flute's homework. By that time Flute was out of bed and feeling pretty good but the doctor said he should stay home from school one more day.

I was feeling pretty good also about visiting Flute. I looked forward to staring out his bedroom window and watching the ocean. It looked different every day. I hadn't noticed that before, the way it changed. And it was fun watching the people walking by on the boardwalk.

"Why don't you stay awhile?" Mrs. Greenwood suggested after I handed Flute the homework. We were standing in the kitchen watching her make some very delicious-looking sandwiches. "Flute's friends from the band are coming over to practice and his father might even get into it today."

Mr. Greenwood was picking at the olives in a bowl on the table. He had Flute's serious dark eyes but when he smiled, the seriousness went away.

"Come on, Allan," Flute said. "You can eat dinner with all of us. You can even hear the new song we're playing for the spring concert before anyone else does."

I heard myself say okay. Then I took an olive from the bowl and ate it.

In about an hour, the bandies arrived. Of course I didn't call them that, but I couldn't help thinking of them as bandies and since no one could hear my thoughts, I felt that was all right. Everyone brought something. There was a drum and a violin and even a harmonica. I was surprised when Beth walked in carrying her horn. She came over to me right away.

"I didn't know you would be here," she said. The way she smiled made me feel as if she was really glad to see me. "I've got to go practice a little," she said. "But I'll be back." Then she went and sat down with the rest of the bandies.

I sat in the living room as if I were at the movies watching a show. Flute's mother and father sat with me while Flute and his friends filled the house with music. The living room had a window looking out over the ocean, too, and sometimes as I listened to the music, it seemed to keep time with the waves that I could see from where I sat on the couch.

Then even Flute's father joined in. He played the piano while the band members played their instruments. Finally, after about an hour of playing the new song for the spring assembly, it was just Flute and his father while the band members sat on the floor around them listening. Flute's dad played the piano and Flute stood there in front of everyone filling the room with his flute music. Flute's father let his fingers just fly over the piano keys. I don't think I could have done that, stand there like that and not be so scared I couldn't move my fingers. I know Tony couldn't have done it either. It was so quiet in the room except for the music and for a minute I felt so peaceful inside, as if everything I was worried about had disappeared.

"Boy, Alex, your mother sure makes great sandwiches," the drummer said.

"Hey, Alex, open up the potato chips will you?" the girl violinist moved closer to Alex, closer than she had to, I thought.

"You really did a good job on that music, Alex," I said. I knew I couldn't call him Flute even though I still thought of him as Flute. I'd call him Alexander sometimes, like when his mother answered the telephone and I said, "Is Alexander home?" I realized everyone in the room thought of him as Alex.

While we were sitting in the living room on the floor on a big tablecloth that Alex's mother had spread out, just as if we were at a picnic, his father handed me a glass of soda.

"You really spent a lot of time helping Alex put together those cars," he said. "I'm glad he has such a good friend as you, Allan. I'm away a lot on the road and I worry about him sometimes. There are a lot of things I'd like to do with him but I can't."

I was thinking about my father and his job and that it was the same way with me. I guess Alex and I had a lot of things that were the same. Even liking sandwiches that were piled high with turkey and mayonnaise.

Even though I didn't talk to any of the bandies in school, they made me feel right at home in

93

Alex's living room. They handed me some potato chips and pretzels, and Beth kept sitting by me in between practice sessions.

"Does everyone in your family have freckles?" she asked me as she got ready to leave.

"Just my dad," I answered, not sure I liked the question.

"I like freckles," she said. "See you tomorrow."

That made me feel better. I wished I had told her my dad had lots of them.

When everyone left, Mr. Greenwood and Flute and I went downstairs to their basement.

"You have to see the car we're working on," Flute's dad said. It was a green Mustang and wasn't easy to put together.

It wasn't easy the next day either to say hello to Flute and all the other band members he sat with who had been at his house the day before, and then walk over to Tony's table and sit down to eat. I didn't eat too well that day. The potato chips stuck in my mouth and the sandwich felt dry even though it was my favorite, peanut butter with creamy marshmallow on top. I didn't say much to Tony or Pete. I just sat there listening to them say stupid things about everyone in the lunchroom including Flute.

That afternoon when I got home, I was surprised to find out that Grandmom Sarah wasn't home. Instead there was a note on the kitchen table.

"Allan, please come to the library and pick me up. I got a ride over. I would appreciate it if you could come and walk me back."

The library was only five blocks away. I made it in no time at all. When I got there, Grandmom was very busy. She was sitting at a round table with stacks of books piled up in front of her.

"I'm cataloging them," she said, talking very low. "They have so much work to do here and so very little help."

I couldn't believe Grandmom was back at work. She looked like she had never left.

"Good-bye, Sarah," the woman at the desk called as Grandmom and I walked to the door. "Can you come back tomorrow?"

"Sure can," Grandmom answered.

"Oh, that's wonderful," the woman smiled. "How about if I drive over on my way to work and bring you in?"

"Oh, that would be fine, Mary," my grandmom said. She was smiling, too, and I realized I hadn't seen her really smile in months, maybe even since Grandpop Harry had died.

I thought Grandmom would be tired when we got home, but she didn't seem to be at all.

"I need your help today, Allan," she said. "We

have a couple of hours until your parents get home. Do you have some free time?"

"Sure," I answered.

For the first time in a couple of weeks, Grandmom headed toward the attic. I was sort of worried about that, that she was falling into her old ways of spending time up there. She walked very slowly up the steps.

"Just walk beside me and hold on to my elbow so I don't lose my balance," she said. "My foot is still a little weak."

That didn't make me feel so good. "Maybe you shouldn't go up there," I told her. Actually I was thinking maybe she should wait until my dad was climbing the steps behind her.

"Nonsense. You're a young man. *You* can do anything I need done."

When we got to the top of the steps, Grandmom pointed to the boxes of books on the floor in the attic.

"Now Allan, could you please carry down that, and that, and those and, over there, that box." She was pointing all over the place, to different parts of the attic. "Be careful. They're not too heavy. I'll wait up here until you're finished. Just please put them in the living room."

It took about a half hour of pulling and pushing and lifting and carrying, but finally, Grandmom and I and seven boxes of books were in the living room.

"What are you going to do with them?" I asked.

"I'm going to look through each box," Grandmom said. "I'm going to pick out the very special books I love and put up some shelves in my room for them. For now I'll just stack them in a corner. The rest I'm going to donate to the library to sell at their book sale. They have a big sale in a few weeks. All the money raised goes to the upkeep of the library, so my books will help."

"I didn't think you'd ever give any of them away," I said, looking down at the books all filled with dust.

"Neither did I, Allan," Grandmom lifted one from the box and started turning the pages. "But, you know, things change. They change even if you don't want them to change. And sometimes you just have to change with them. I had plenty of time to think while I was stuck in this house. What good are all these books if no one gets to read them. What good are they in the attic?"

And then Grandmom Sarah took my hand and held it for a minute in hers. "I guess I finally had to decide that this is my home now, Allan, and Ocean View is where I live. I guess I just had to make a decision about how I was going to live, and if I was going to spend the rest of my life looking back in the attic, instead of looking forward."

While I watched Grandmom stack the books, one pile for the library, one pile for her, I wondered if I was doing the same thing, looking back too much and not moving forward.

10

I knew it was a beach day as soon as I got up in the morning. Even though it was only the end of May, the sun was hot coming into my room, and even though my window was wide open, there wasn't any cool air coming in.

The telephone rang. I heard my mother answer it in her room.

"It's for you, Allan," she said.

I ran into my parents' bedroom and jumped on the bed.

"Hi, Allan. Want to do something today?" It was Flute.

"What do you want to do?" I asked.

"Oh, I don't know. Maybe race our cars in your driveway. Later, we could go to the beach."

"Okay," I answered. "Bring over the Porsche."

It was Saturday and my mom and I had an agreement that on Saturday I clean up my room. That's where Flute found me when he got to my house.

"I'll be done in a minute," I told him. "I've just got to look under the bed and see if I've left anything there."

I usually did. Maybe a couple of socks or my underwear or a few pencils. I never knew how they got under the bed. *I* certainly didn't put them there.

When I pulled out a school notebook I had been looking for all week, I found Flute holding my bear. I had forgotten to put it away in the closet.

"I have one of these," Flute said. "Mine's brown. I call him Little Guy. The stuffing is coming out of him, I've had him so long." Flute carefully put the bear back on the bureau.

I guess it was then that I knew I wouldn't have to explain to Flute about the bear, or Grandpop Harry, or even throw the bear in the closet. I guess I knew then that there would be a lot of things Flute would understand that Tony never would. Maybe on Monday I would sit in the lunchroom with Flute and his friends and Beth with the silver-blonde hair.

We raced the cars in the driveway for about an hour. But it was too nice to stay away from the beach. We could hear the ocean even from where we were, and the air had a fishy smell to it.

"I have two fishing rods in the garage," I told Flute. "Want to go down to the beach and fish off the jetty?"

"Sure," Flute answered.

We got the rods and my fishing box. I took some blood worms that I kept in a small white cardboard box in the refrigerator and we were just about to walk out on the porch when Grandmom caught up with us. She rushed out from her bedroom dressed in her library clothes, a white blouse and a skirt and even stockings and dressy shoes.

"Do me a favor, Allan," she said. "I have a meeting with the mayor today. I'll tell you about it when I get back. But I haven't fed the ducks and I just don't have time. Take this over, will you be a dear?" She plunked a brown bag of corn seed into my hands.

"We were going to the beach," I told Grandmom Sarah. I hadn't been to Silver Lake for a couple of days, because the weather was getting better and there was more to do after school, like play basketball with Flute in his driveway. Anyway, I knew Grandmom was taking good care of the ducks. She was walking really well now and I thought she enjoyed feeding the ducks as much as they loved eating.

"That's okay," Flute said. "I like feeding the ducks. It won't take long."

We were about one block from the lake when I heard the honking. There was no doubt about it. It was the honking of geese. I walked a little faster.

101

It was as if they knew we were coming. All the birds on the lake were excited, some of them flying overhead, others waddling back and forth on the slope going down to the lake. By this time, I guess they knew me. Evelyn and Al were crossing the street, slowing down traffic as usual as they hurried toward us. In the middle, walking between them, was Snowbird. I gave Flute some corn seed and he stood there feeding the ducks that had gathered around him.

I bent down and put some corn into my hand. Evelyn and Al came right over as if they knew what they were supposed to do. They ate it right from my hand, pecking away carefully so they wouldn't hurt me, as if we were old friends.

"Come on, Snowbird," I said gently. I knew I didn't have to be afraid to talk in front of Flute, almost the way I used to be able to say anything to David. "I won't hurt you, Snowbird, I promise."

The little duck came over carefully and wedged herself between Evelyn and Al. The three of them ate out of my hands. I felt Snowbird had forgiven me, but more important, I felt she wasn't alone anymore. Evelyn and Al seemed to be her new friends, and they were doing a good job protecting her. When they were finished eating, the three of them rested under the willow tree.

By the time we got done, there must have been over fifty ducks, green-necked mallards, a few sea gulls, all walking around the side of the lake. They didn't leave much corn seed behind, and when we left them they were sunning themselves along the side of the water.

We had just passed the bridge, heading toward the boardwalk, when I heard the geese honking again. But it wasn't the same kind of honking. There was something frightening about it. It was loud and over and over as if Evelyn or Al were scared or in trouble.

"What's wrong?" Flute asked as I turned and looked back.

"I don't know," I said. "But I think something's wrong back there. Could we go back and see?"

"Sure," Flute answered, and we ran toward the sound that was getting louder and louder.

It didn't take long to see Tony and Pete running along the side of the lake, throwing their pebbles into the water. Evelyn and Al were fighting back. Instead of running, they stood in front of Snowbird, protecting her. Big Al spread his wings and flapped them angrily at Tony, and even Evelyn had a few things to say.

"What are they doing that for?" Flute asked. "They could hurt the ducks!" I had never seen him angry. I realized that now because his dark eyes frightened me.

Flute and I didn't tell each other what we were going to do. I guess we both just knew what had to be done. We laid our fishing rods on the ground and ran toward Tony and Pete. It was one of those times where talking wouldn't do any good. I had tried it, and I guess Flute didn't even think about it. He just took a flying leap and tackled Pete. I was smaller than Tony but when I took hold of his legs and felt him lose his balance, I was thinking about a lot of things that made me stronger. I was thinking about all the weeks I had been feeling alone in Ocean View and I was thinking about how tough Tony had made it for me. I was thinking about the male snowbird that wouldn't see the way the flowers were growing all around the lake this spring, and I was thinking about the female snowbird who might have to move away because she was in danger here at the lake.

We rolled around on the ground. I tasted some dirt in my mouth when Tony pushed my face down into it. I heard him breathing real hard while he was sitting on top of me, right on my back. I looked up, laying there on my stomach, and saw Snowbird standing a few feet away, looking down at me. The geese stood next to her, flapping their wings. Well, I knew I couldn't lose this fight, not in front of Snowbird and Big Al and Evelyn. It would be too embarrassing. I flipped over real fast, the way the wrestlers do on television, and pinned Tony on his back.

"I don't want to see you hurting those ducks

anymore," Flute yelled while he shoved Pete away from the lake.

"Me neither," I said, looking Tony squarely in the eye.

Tony didn't say much when I finally let him up. He dusted himself off and just looked at me as if we were meeting for the first time. And I guess we were.

Before he left, Tony yelled, "What are you going to do, Allan, sit here with Flute and guard the ducks all day?"

I left Snowbird with Evelyn and Al, thinking about what Tony had said. He was right. We couldn't be here all the time. Who would guard Snowbird when we were at school, or busy after school? Maybe they couldn't be safe here anymore. Maybe Evelyn and Al knew something I was just finding out, that they had to take Snowbird away in order for her to survive.

I didn't know it then, but I had nothing to worry about. Grandmom Sarah took care of everything. Two days later, when Flute and I had come home from school and were going to do our plant project together, Grandmom Sarah was waiting for us.

"Come on out to the lake," she said, hurrying us out the door. "I've been waiting for you. I've got a surprise for you, Allan."

As we approached the lake, everything looked the same to me. Some of the mallards were gathered by the little green house, pecking away at leftover food on the ground. A lot of the birds were cleaning themselves. Evelyn and Al were sitting on the bridge with Snowbird between them. It was then that I saw what was standing in front of the bridge. There was a large sign posted there:

GEESE CROSSING
DRIVE WITH CAUTION
ANYONE SEEN THROWING ANYTHING HARMFUL
AT THE BIRDS IN THIS LAKE
WILL BE FINED $500
KEEP THIS LAKE CLEAN
LITTERERS WILL ALSO BE FINED
WE LOVE OUR BIRDS

The print was big, so big you could see it from across the street. There were two signs, as Grandmom pointed out. One was on the other side of the lake, in Sea Bright.

"I had a long talk with the mayor," Grandmom Sarah said, standing proudly by the sign as if she had printed it herself. "And then we had a township meeting and everyone voted on keeping these birds as safe as possible. They bring a lot of beauty to Ocean View and we don't want to lose them."

That night I called David. He was really glad to hear from me.

"Is it okay if I come out next weekend?" he asked.

"Sure," I answered. "I've got a new friend I want you to meet. His name is Alex. Bring your model cars so we can all race them in the driveway."

Before I went to sleep that night, I looked out the window toward the lake. All I could hear were the crickets talking to one another, but I knew Snowbird was ending her day, too. I also knew I didn't have to worry about her anymore. Maybe she couldn't read the sign that protected her and all the other birds who lived on the lake. But she would feel the love from all of us who wanted her to stay. Ocean View wasn't such a bad town to live in after all.

APPLE°PAPERBACKS

Pick an Apple and Polish Off Some Great Reading!

NEW APPLE TITLES

☐	MT43356-3	Family Picture Dean Hughes	$2.75
☐	MT41682-0	Dear Dad, Love Laurie Susan Beth Pfeffer	$2.75
☐	MT41529-8	My Sister, the Creep	
		Candice F. Ransom	$2.75

BESTSELLING APPLE TITLES

☐	MT42709-1	Christina's Ghost Betty Ren Wright	$2.75
☐	MT43461-6	The Dollhouse Murders Betty Ren Wright	$2.75
☐	MT42319-3	The Friendship Pact Susan Beth Pfeffer	$2.75
☐	MT43444-6	Ghosts Beneath Our Feet Betty Ren Wright	$2.75
☐	MT40605-1	Help! I'm a Prisoner in the Library Eth Clifford	$2.50
☐	MT42193-X	Leah's Song Eth Clifford	$2.50
☐	MT43618-X	Me and Katie (The Pest) Ann M. Martin	$2.75
☐	MT42883-7	Sixth Grade Can Really Kill You Barthe DeClements	$2.75
☐	MT40409-1	Sixth Grade Secrets Louis Sachar	$2.75
☐	MT42882-9	Sixth Grade Sleepover Eve Bunting	$2.75
☐	MT41732-0	Too Many Murphys	
		Colleen O'Shaughnessy McKenna	$2.75
☐	MT41118-7	Tough-Luck Karen Johanna Hurwitz	$2.50
☐	MT42326-6	Veronica the Show-off Nancy K. Robinson	$2.75

Available wherever you buy books...or use the coupon below.

- -

Scholastic Inc., P.O. Box 7502, 2932 East McCarty Street, Jefferson City, MO 65102

Please send me the books I have checked above. I am enclosing $_____ (please add $2.00 to cover shipping and handling). Send check or money order — no cash or C.O.D.'s please.

Name_____

Address_____

City _____ State/Zip _____

Please allow four to six weeks for delivery. Offer good in the U.S.A. only.
Sorry, mail orders are not available to residents of Canada. Prices subject to change.

APP1089